To all my imaginary friends. I love you guys

Tundra Books, an imprint of Penguin Random House Canada Young Readers,
a division of Penguin Random House of Canada Limited

Library and Archives Canada Cataloguing in Publication

Title: The unforgettable party / Noemi Vola.
Names: Vola, Noemi, 1993- author, illustrator.
Description: Written by the author in Italian, but not published. First published in English.
Identifiers: Canadiana (print) 20200290290 | Canadiana (ebook) 20200290304
ISBN 9780735270909 (hardcover) | ISBN 9780735270916 (EPUB)
Classification: LCC PZ7.1.V65 U54 2021 | DDC j853/.92—dc23

Published simultaneously in the United States of America by Tundra Books of Northern
New York, an imprint of Penguin Random House Canada Young Readers,
a division of Penguin Random House of Canada Limited

Library of Congress Control Number: 2020941843

Edited by Peter Phillips
Translated by Debbie Bibo
Designed by John Martz
The artwork in this book was rendered digitally.
The text was set in Worcester Round.

Printed in China

www.penguinrandomhouse.ca

1 2 3 4 5   25 24 23 22 21

Penguin
Random House
tundra   TUNDRA BOOKS

NOEMI VOLA

THE UNFORGETTABLE PARTY

tundra

Caterpillar was bored.

He had read all of the books
on his bookshelf . . .

and found all of the partners
for his missing socks.

Enough was enough.
Caterpillar decided to throw a party.

He already had everything he needed:

APPLE JUICE

CONFETTI

DECORATIONS

DESSERT

PARTY HATS

PIZZA

STAR STICKERS TO STICK ON YOUR FACE

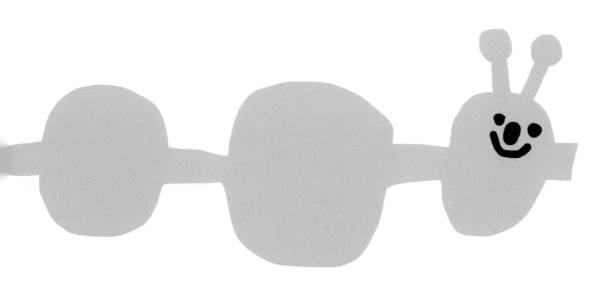

He had a house that was large and empty . . .

and neighbors who didn't mind the noise.

Everything was perfect, except for one missing ingredient: friends! Caterpillar tried to invite some . . .

but everyone was, um, busy.

Oh, he was so sad.

I'M SO SAD.

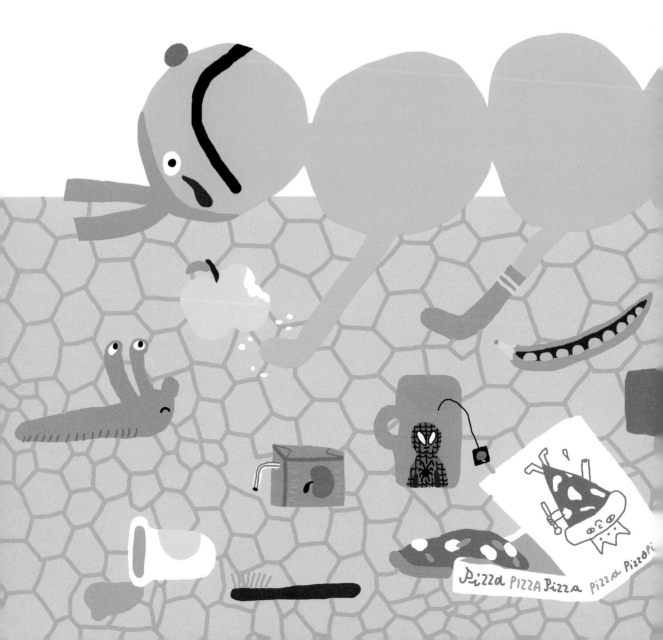

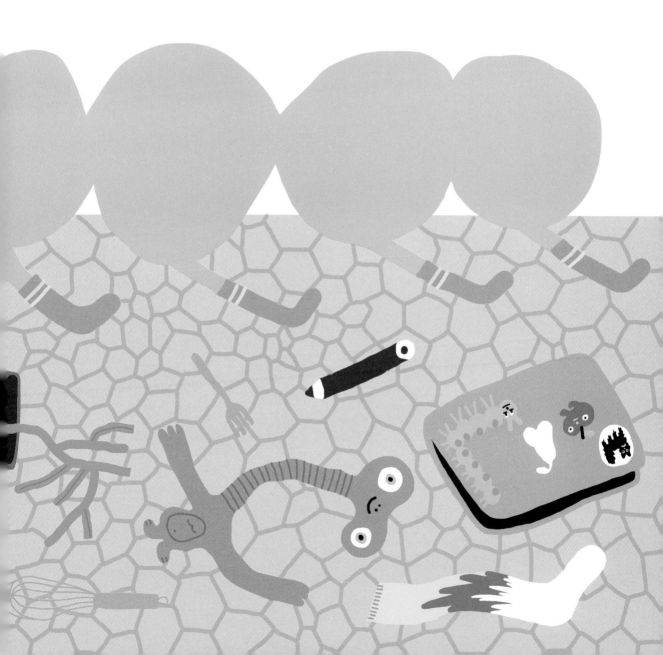

There just *had* to be a solution!
So Caterpillar did some research.

He couldn't find anything . . .

so he started to think.

He thought all day.

Then, finally, Caterpillar came up with a plan.

WHY, OF COURSE!!!
WHAT A BRILLIANT IDEA!

Now Caterpillar wasn't alone anymore!
He made six new friends, all very different,
fun, interesting and with lots of character.
Their names were:

PEPPI

PULLI

PALLI

PILLI

PIPPI

PHILIP

And then there's Caterpillar,
but we already know him.

After they introduced
themselves and shook
each other's feet,
it was time for the
party to begin.

And so the celebration began.

They danced . . .

and played.

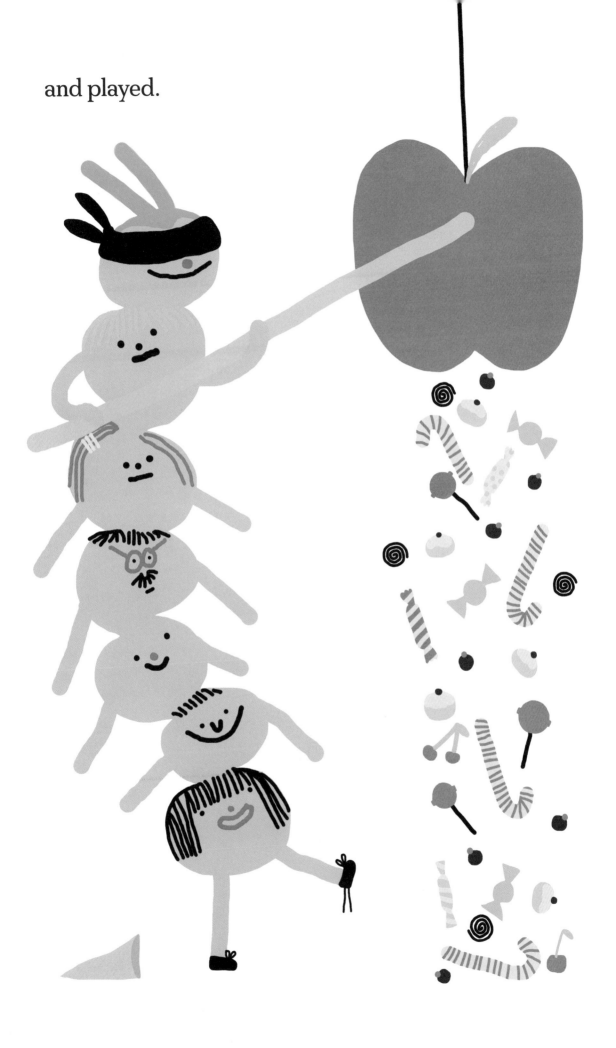

They ate seven feet of pizza,

sang the theme songs from their
favorite cartoons,

put on costumes

and romped around
until it was morning.

It was a marvelous party.
Exhausted, they all fell asleep
on the couch.

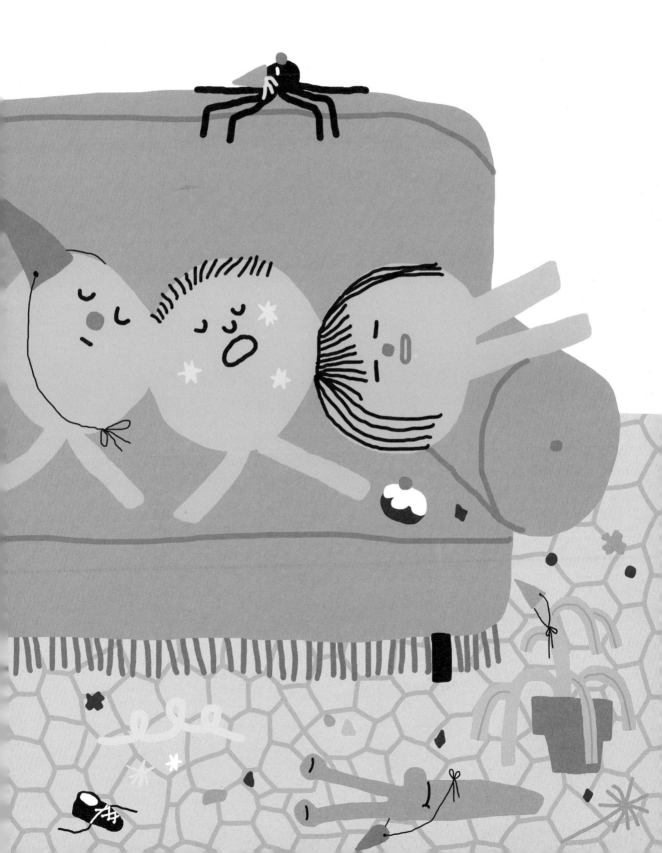

That night, Caterpillar had a terrible
nightmare. He dreamed that Pulli, Peppi,
Pilli, Palli, Pippi and Philip decided to
leave. Each one went to a different place.

I'M GOING TO
THE BEACH.

I WANT TO
STAY IN A HOTEL.

I'M GOING TO
LIVE AT THE TOP
OF A VOLCANO !

I'M GOING
TO FINLAND.

They left by taxi, by bike, by skateboard,
by bus, by airplane and even by duck.
Caterpillar was afraid he'd never see them again.

PERHAPS. LET'S SEE
HOW THINGS GO.

Caterpillar was alone. He couldn't even
move because his new friends took his
legs when they left.

He had to stand on his antennae, and
when he walked, he saw the whole world
upside down!

Caterpillar awoke with a start
and a terrible headache!

He was sweating, and his
heart was pounding.

Fortunately, his friends hadn't noticed anything. They were still there, sleeping nearby.

Caterpillar took advantage of the fact that they were sleeping to go and take a bath. He walked on his tiptoes so as not to wake them up and slipped into the tub.

"It was such a marvelous party. I won't ever forget it," he said. Then he thought about inviting them to stay for breakfast.